W9-BZA-748

SUPER
SPECIAL
#3

SUBWAY SERIES SURPRISE

BALLPARK MYSTERIES®

Also by David A. Kelly
THE MVP SERIES

Babe Ruth and the Baseball Curse

SUPER
SPECIAL
#3

SUBWAY
SERIES
SURPRISE

by David A. Kelly

illustrated by Mark Meyers

A STEPPING STONE BOOK™
Random House 🏠 New York

This book is dedicated to my wife, Alice Lesch Kelly, an original Mets fan and fellow native New Yorker, who always knows how to help make Mike and Kate better detectives and the Ballpark Mysteries more mysterious.
—D.A.K.

"It ain't over till it's over."
—Yogi Berra, an eighteen-time MLB All-Star, and player, manager, and coach over the years of both the New York Yankees and New York Mets

This is a work of fiction. Names, characters, places, and incidents either are the product of the author's imagination or are used fictitiously. Any resemblance to actual persons, living or dead, events, or locales is entirely coincidental.

Text copyright © 2018 by David A. Kelly
Cover art and interior illustrations copyright © 2018 by Mark Meyers

All rights reserved. Published in the United States by Random House Children's Books, a division of Penguin Random House LLC, New York.

Random House and the colophon are registered trademarks and A Stepping Stone Book and the colophon are trademarks of Penguin Random House LLC. Ballpark Mysteries® is a registered trademark of Upside Research, Inc.

Visit us on the Web!
SteppingStonesBooks.com
rhcbooks.com

Educators and librarians, for a variety of teaching tools, visit us at
RHTeachersLibrarians.com

Library of Congress Cataloging-in-Publication Data
Names: Kelly, David A., author. | Meyers, Mark, illustrator.
Title: Subway Series surprise / by David A. Kelly ; illustrated by Mark Meyers.
Description: New York : Random House, [2018] | Series: Ballpark mysteries. Super special ; #3 | "A Stepping Stone book." | Summary: In New York City for the annual series between rival teams, the Yankees and the Mets, Mike and Kate investigate a spate of pranks, thefts, and sabotage.
Identifiers: LCCN 2017048866 | ISBN 978-0-525-57892-5 (trade) | ISBN 978-0-525-57893-2 (lib. bdg.) | ISBN 978-0-525-57894-9 (ebook)
Subjects: CYAC: Baseball—Fiction. | Conduct of life—Fiction. | New York Mets (Baseball team)—Fiction. | New York Yankees (Baseball team)—Fiction. | Mystery and detective stories.
Classification: LCC PZ7.K2936 Su 2018 | DDC [Fic]—dc23

Printed in the United States of America
10 9 8 7 6 5 4 3 2 1

This book has been officially leveled by using the F&P Text Level Gradient™ Leveling System.

Random House Children's Books supports the First Amendment and celebrates the right to read.

Contents

Mets vs. Yankees

Mike Walsh and his cousin Kate Hopkins stood on the sidelines of the Brooklyn Cyclones minor-league baseball game. It was the seventh-inning stretch, and they had an important job to do.

"Bring out the hot dogs!" said a man standing near the pitcher's mound. He wore a straw hat and bright blue jacket. "It's Mets fans versus Yankees fans in the Subway Series Hot-Dog-Eating Contest!"

"We got 'em!" Kate called back as thousands

of fans in the stadium cheered. Kate and Mike rushed across the Cyclones' infield, carrying huge trays of Nathan's Famous hot dogs.

They were headed for the two long tables on either side of the announcer. Behind each table were three Mets or Yankees fans chosen from the crowd.

Kate ran up to the table on the left. Two women and a man, each wearing blue and orange Mets shirts, sat behind it. At the front of the table was a big banner that read GO, METS! Kate placed ten hot dogs in front of each competitor. "Good luck!" she said to the three contestants. "Try to eat fast! I want one of the Mets fans to win!"

"And I want a Yankees fan to win!" Mike called from the other table. The sign on that table read GO, YANKEES! Mike had placed ten hot dogs in front of each person on his side.

The contestants were each wearing pin-striped Yankees jerseys. The crowd cheered.

Mike and Kate met near the third-base line to watch. It was Friday afternoon, and they were in New York City for a big Subway Series between the Mets and the Yankees that started that night. The teams would be playing each other three times in the next three days.

The games were called a Subway Series because fans could reach both the Mets' and the Yankees' stadiums using the New York City subway. Before the Los Angeles Dodgers and San Francisco Giants moved to California from New York in the 1950s, they had also played the New York Yankees in Subway Series games.

Kate's mom had driven Mike and Kate down to New York City from their homes in Cooperstown, New York, the day before. She was a sports reporter and was in the press box working. Mrs. Hopkins had arranged for Mike and Kate to be part of the Cyclones' hot-dog-eating contest.

The Cyclones were a minor-league team for the New York Mets. Their stadium was right next to the ocean, in the neighborhood of Coney Island in Brooklyn, New York. During the summer, lots of people in New York City went to Coney Island for fun. Nearby was a wide wooden boardwalk with rides, games, and food stands. Roller coasters zipped back and forth just beyond the stadium's outfield wall, and waves broke on the sandy beach outside the ballpark.

The announcer running the contest waved his straw hat in the air. "Whoever eats the most hot dogs wins four front-row seats to all Subway Series games!" he said.

Mike nudged Kate with his elbow. He rubbed his stomach in a circular motion. "I'll bet I could eat the most hot dogs if they'd let me," he said.

Kate shook her head. Her brown ponytail bobbed back and forth through the hole in her blue baseball cap. "It's only for adults!" she said. "But let's buy some hot dogs when we're done!"

Ball boys and girls finished bringing out bottles of ketchup, mustard, and relish and placed big jugs of water on the tables. According to the rules, the contestants could eat the hot dogs plain or with condiments, but they also had to eat the buns.

Behind the tables, the contestants prepared to eat. Some took swigs of water. Others slathered their hot dogs with mustard or relish. One woman rolled her head from side to side and made chewing motions with her jaw. A man rubbed his belly and took deep breaths.

Mike glanced at Kate. "I'm rooting for the Yankees fans to win," he said. "Because Babe Ruth played for them."

"Well, I'm rooting for the Mets side because my father likes them," Kate said. Her parents were divorced. Kate's father lived in Los Angeles.

"Why not root for the Yankees, like your mom?" Mike asked.

"Because my dad works for the Dodgers!" Kate said. "After both the Brooklyn Dodgers and the New York Giants moved to California in the 1950s, the Yankees were the only base-ball team left in New York. So when Major League Baseball created the Mets in 1962, they wanted to honor the memory of the Giants and the Dodgers."

Kate pointed to a Mets logo on her program.

It was a round logo that showed the outline of a bridge in front of a bunch of city buildings. "See how the Mets logo is blue and orange?"

"Um, yeah," Mike said. "What's that got to do with anything?"

"It's actually *Dodger* blue and *Giants* orange!" Kate said. "The Mets used colors from the old Brooklyn Dodgers and New York Giants for their uniforms and logos!"

The announcer counted down for the start of the contest. "Five . . . four . . . three . . . two . . . one . . . HOT DOGS!" he yelled.

The Mets and Yankees fans behind the tables stuffed one hot dog after another into their mouths. Some dipped the hot dogs in water and swallowed them in two bites, and then stuffed the rolls in separately. Others simply took big bites of the hot dogs with the buns. Some put mustard on them, but most didn't.

"One minute left!" the announcer yelled.

More hot dogs disappeared from the table. A few contestants had stopped and were holding their stomachs as if they felt sick.

"METS! METS! METS! METS!" the crowd chanted. In the background, roller coasters zoomed up and down as their riders screamed.

The announcer checked his watch and held up his hand. "Five ... four ... three ... two ... one ... STOP!" he yelled. He swung his hand to end the contest. "Put down your hot dogs! Take your last swallow."

"Who won?" Kate asked.

The announcer walked from one end of the tables to the other. He counted the leftover hot dogs in front of each person. Then he turned to the crowd.

"We have a winner with NINE hot dogs eaten!" he said.

"Come on, Yankees!" Mike said.

"Let's go, Mets!" Kate said.

The announcer glanced back at both tables. It seemed like he was counting the hot dogs one more time. He turned to the crowd. "The winner of this year's free tickets will be rooting for the . . ."

A Mysterious
Mets Fan

The announcer paused.

The fans clapped and cheered for their favorite sides.

"Which team?" Mike yelled.

"METS! METS! METS!" chanted the fans in the first row of seats.

"Who won the free tickets?" Kate asked.

The announcer held up his hand. "The winner of the hot-dog-eating contest will be rooting for the METS *and* the YANKEES!" he called. "This year we have a TIE!"

"What?" Kate and Mike asked at the same time.

"Ladies and gentlemen!" the announcer said. "We have a first! It's a tie! One person on *both* the Mets and Yankees sides ate nine hot dogs! That means we'll split up the four tickets. Each person who ate nine hot dogs will get two box seats for the Subway Series games. Congratulations!"

A man on the Yankees side and a woman from the Mets side held up their hands in victory. The crowd cheered as they waved.

"A tie? Are you kidding me?" Kate said. "There are no ties in baseball!"

Mike shook his head. "Well, except for that one all-star game in 2002," he said. "And I think there was another tie in 1961. . . ."

"Not today!" Kate said. "I know how to break that tie. I'm challenging you to our *own* hot-dog-eating contest. Mike versus Kate. We'll see who can eat the most!"

Mike laughed. "You know me—I'm always hungry," he said. "Hungry for hot dogs. And hungry to win a contest!"

"We'll see about that," Kate said. She gave Mike's shirt a tug. "Let's go get some hot dogs. Then we can go find my mom after the game. She's interviewing people for her book on Subway Series heroes."

Mike followed Kate as she ran off the field. Behind them, the batboys and batgirls carried the hot-dog tables away. The Brooklyn Cyclones warmed up on the sidelines, waiting to take their turn at bat.

The main walkway was crowded with people heading back to their seats. At the top of the stairs, Kate stopped to look for the nearest food stand. She spotted one to their right. But before she could head for it, someone tapped her on the shoulder.

Kate whirled around.

It was a hot-dog vendor! The woman had a big box of hot dogs on a strap around her neck. "Ah! Just the two I was looking for!" she said. "I saw you helping with the contest. You did a great job."

"Thanks!" Mike said. "It was fun."

She pulled out two hot dogs and wrapped them in napkins. "Here are some hot dogs for helping," she said. She handed one to Mike and one to Kate. She also gave them some mustard and relish packets.

"Enjoy!" She waved goodbye and walked away.

Mike ripped open the foil package. "How cool is that?" he asked. "Free food for doing a good job!" He squeezed mustard and relish onto his hot dog.

As Kate started to unwrap her hot dog, she noticed some black marks on the napkin. When she looked closer, she couldn't believe her eyes. There was a message on her napkin!

"Mike! Look at this!" she said.

"Grrmph!" he sputtered. Mike had just taken a bite.

Kate read aloud:

Kate (and Mike!):

Think you're good at solving mysteries?
Try this one:
  I'm not here, but I'm here.
  You don't see me now, but I saw you.
  Meet me at the monuments with your mom
  when the subways meet a second time.
  And I'll give you something special
  if you give me something special.

"Whoa! What does that mean?" Mike asked.

"I don't know!" Kate said. "We've got to find

that hot-dog lady!" She scanned the walkway. "There she is! Quick!"

They took off running. When they caught up to the hot-dog vendor, she was about to head into a stockroom. "Hey! Excuse me!" Kate said.

The woman turned around. "Oh! It's you two," she said.

Kate waved the napkin in front of her. "Where did you get this napkin? Who gave it to you?" she asked.

The woman shrugged. "A guy in a Mets jersey," she said. "He paid for two hot dogs at the start of the game, but he asked me to wait and give them to you with the note after the contest. He said he had to get back to the stadium, but he wanted to leave them for you."

"What did he look like?" Kate asked. "What was his name?"

"He didn't say," she said as she opened the door to the stockroom. "He was average size, dark hair. He was wearing sunglasses. He also had a silver watch with a blue and white band. But there was one strange thing about him. He had a blue Mets jersey on, but he was wearing a Yankees baseball hat! That's all I know! I gotta go now! Bye!"

"But we need to find him!" Kate said.

Another Mystery

BANG!

The door of the stockroom slammed shut. The hot-dog lady was gone.

Mike clapped his hands. "So, we just need to find the guy in the Mets jersey!" he said.

"Mike! Look around!" Kate said. She waved her arm at the fans streaming by them. "The Cyclones are a Mets farm team! Almost *everyone* here is wearing a Mets jersey!"

Mike turned and glanced at the fans nearby. Then he blushed and shrugged. "Well, maybe that's good," he said. "It gives us a lot of suspects to follow up on!"

Kate shook her head. "Are you kidding?" she asked. "We can't solve a mystery if *everyone* is a suspect. We need to figure out who dropped that note off."

Mike snapped his fingers. "What if it wasn't a Mets fan?" he asked. "What if the sunglasses and jersey were just a disguise? He could be a Yankees fan."

Kate nodded. "Maybe . . . ," she said. "But then who was he and why is he asking us to solve a mystery?"

Mike shrugged again. "I don't know," he said. "I think my brain needs some food!" He unwrapped the rest of his hot dog and took another bite. Kate did the same. "Mmm, mmm," Mike said when he finished. "Free food always tastes good to me!"

"Kate! Mike!" a woman's voice called.

Kate's mom was running down the main hallway. She wore a blue baseball hat with a ponytail hanging out the back. She had a black messenger bag slung over her shoulder.

"I'm so glad I found you!" she said as she stopped in front of them. "I've been looking for the past ten minutes."

"What's up?" Kate asked. "The game's not over."

Kate's mom nodded. "Something important came up," she said. "We've got to get over to the Mets' stadium early. Someone broke into the press box!"

"Oh no!" Kate said. "I hope your research wasn't stolen!" Mrs. Hopkins had spent the morning working in the press box.

"Me too!" Kate's mom said. "I have to finish my Subway Series book by next month. If my notes and interviews were stolen, I don't know what I'll do!"

Outside the stadium, Mrs. Hopkins flagged down a taxi. She asked the driver to hurry to the Mets' ballpark. When they arrived, Mike and Kate hopped out as Mrs. Hopkins paid.

VOOOOOOOOOOOMMMMM!

Mike and Kate covered their ears and

looked up. A large airplane streaked across the sky over the stadium.

Mrs. Hopkins stepped out of the car. "Oh, I forgot to tell you," she said as the noise quieted down. "The Mets' stadium is right near LaGuardia Airport! Planes fly over all the time."

Mike watched the plane disappear into some puffy white clouds. "That reminds me," he said to Kate. "Have you heard the joke about the airplane?"

Kate squiggled her eyebrows. "Nooo . . . ," she said.

Mike waved his hand. "Ah, well, don't worry. It was over your head anyway!"

"Ha-ha," Kate said. "Very funny."

"Come on," Mrs. Hopkins said. "We have got to check out the break-in." She led them to the main entrance. Mrs. Hopkins showed the security guard her press pass. He waved them in.

They wound through the stadium, up to the press box. Inside were rows of tiered seats facing large windows overlooking the field. The reporters had a great view.

"Oh! I'm glad you're here to examine your stuff, Laura," said another reporter. He was wearing tan pants, a white shirt, and a Mets baseball cap. "We don't know who broke in here or why, but the Mets security team is checking different areas in the stadium."

The man motioned to a security guard taking pictures. "If anything of yours is missing, tell her," he said. "That's Emma. She's leading the investigation. Nothing of mine is missing, but the thief took books and notes from the desks next to yours."

"Thanks, Milo," Mrs. Hopkins said. "I hope everything is okay. Mike and Kate, this is my friend Milo. He's also a sports reporter. Watch out, though, because he works for a rival website. But he's still a pretty good guy."

"Don't listen to her," Milo said with a laugh. "She's just jealous because sometimes I get the scoop on news stories before she does!"

Mike and Kate said hello to Milo, and then followed Mrs. Hopkins to her desk. A pile of baseball books sat on one side. Nearby were a notebook and a pen. Mrs. Hopkins picked up the notebook.

She studied it for a moment, and then dropped it on the desk.

"Oh no!" Mrs. Hopkins said. "It's empty! Someone took my research notes!"

Decoding the Note

Kate picked up the notebook. There was nothing inside but a few sheets of blank paper.

"Didn't you have a copy of them?" she asked. "Or a backup on your computer?"

Kate's mother slumped into the chair next to the desk. She shook her head. "No!" she said. "I haven't had a chance to make a copy. And I didn't record the interviews, either. If I don't get my notes back, I won't be able to finish the book!"

"Maybe Mike and I can help find them!" Kate said.

Her mom looked at her and sighed. "Thanks," she said. "I'd be happy to have your help." Mrs. Hopkins looked at Emma, the guard. "And yours, too!"

"We are already checking things out," Emma said. "We reviewed the security video from the hallway and have a suspect. A man went into the press box at three o'clock today. He left a few minutes later, but he wasn't carrying anything. We don't know if he was the thief, but we suspect it."

"Could you see what he looked like from the video?" Mike asked.

"We couldn't see his face," Emma said. "But he was wearing a Mets jersey and a Yankees baseball hat."

Mike and Kate glanced at each other. "Did you hear that?" Kate whispered. "Maybe it's the same person who left us the note with the hot dogs!"

Mike nodded.

Emma continued. "Milo showed up an hour after the thief was here and noticed some of the reporters' stuff was moved, so he called us," she said. "Let me know what you're missing, Mrs. Hopkins, and we'll try to find it."

While Mrs. Hopkins was describing what had been stolen, Kate pointed to the other side of the press box. "Let's take another look at that note. We can talk over there," she said. Mike followed her to an empty table.

"It's probably the same person," Mike said as they walked. "The timing works out. The thief left the note for us around one o'clock at the Cyclones game. That means he could have made it over here to the stadium by three o'clock to steal your mom's notes."

Kate nodded. She dug out the napkin. She and Mike studied the message on it.

Kate (and Mike!):

Think you're good at solving mysteries?
Try this one:
  I'm not here, but I'm here.
  You don't see me now, but I saw you.
  Meet me at the monuments with your mom
  when the subways meet a second time.
  And I'll give you something special
  if you give me something special.

Kate pointed to the fifth line. "What about this line: '*You don't see me now, but I saw you*'?" she asked. "That's a little creepy!"

"Yeah, but maybe it just means the person who wrote it saw us handing out hot dogs at the Cyclones game," Mike said. "Besides, whoever it is wants to meet us *and* your mom, so that's okay! I'll bet they want her to pay a big ransom for the stolen notes!"

Kate nodded. " '*Meet me at the monuments with your mom*,'" she read. "What are the monuments? There are lots of important buildings in New York City, like the Empire State Building, but no big monuments like in Washington, D.C."

Mike thought for a moment. "Look at the next line. '*When the subways meet a second time*,'" he said. "I think that means the second game in the Subway Series! The Mets are on the number 7 subway line, and you can reach the Yankees on the number 4, B, or D subway lines. And the second game is at Yankee Stadium tomorrow night!"

"But there aren't any national monuments at Yankee Stadium!" Kate said. "Where are we supposed to meet him?"

"I don't know," Mike said. "Maybe the Statue of Liberty's a national monument. It could mean that."

Kate shook her head. "But the Statue of Liberty isn't near Yankee Stadium. That doesn't make any sense."

They both stared at the paper for a couple of minutes. Mike read it over and over to himself. Suddenly, he jumped up and tapped the note.

"Ooh, ooh!" he said. "It doesn't mean a national monument. Don't you remember from the last time we were there? It means to meet

the thief in Yankee Stadium at *Monument Park*!"

Kate's eyes opened wide. "That's it!" she said. "Monument Park, behind the Yankees' outfield! That's where they have all the retired numbers and plaques for important Yankees players and managers."

Mike nodded. "We meet him there with your mother, and she'll get her notes back!" he said.

"But the note says only if we turn over something special," Kate said. "I'll bet that means a lot of money!"

Mike looked around. The press box was starting to fill up with reporters.

"We should tell your mom," Mike said. "And then maybe we can get some food and watch the game from up here!"

They headed back to the other side of the press box. Kate's mom was working at her desk. A few seats over, Milo was typing on his computer. As they approached, Mike held out his hand to stop Kate.

"What's up?" Kate asked.

"Look over there," Mike whispered. He pointed to a plastic bag hanging from Milo's chair. "Maybe we've found our thief!"

Poking out of the top of the bag was a Yankees baseball cap!

"It can't be Milo!" Kate said. "He's a good friend of my mom's!"

"But he's a rival reporter!" Mike said. "Your mom even said that. He probably doesn't want her to finish the book. He had access to the press box. He has a Yankees hat. He could have faked the robbery and then reported it to security afterward."

"Okay," Kate said. "We can tell my mom about the note later. Let's hang out here to watch the game. That way we can keep an eye on Milo and maybe even find a chance to search his bag for my mom's notes!"

An Apple for the Yankees

"NEW YORK CITY! WELCOME TO THIS YEAR'S SUBWAY SEEEEEEEEERIES!" the announcer boomed. The fans exploded with cheers and claps.

Mike and Kate had gone to get dinner and returned to the press box just in time for the start of the game. On the way back, Mike had bought a baseball with a Mets logo on it. He always liked to have a baseball with him at ballparks in case he had a chance to get a player's signature.

The Mets fans cheered when their team ran out and took the field. And the Yankees fans cheered as their leadoff hitter walked to the plate. Then the Yankees fans cheered even louder when he hit a line drive and ran to second base!

As the runner stopped, the Mets catcher ran out to his pitcher. They covered their mouths

with their gloves and talked for a few minutes before the catcher ran back to home plate.

"Let's go, Mets!" the fans cheered.

The Mets pitcher struck out the next three batters. The first half of the inning was over without the Yankees getting a run.

As they waited for the Yankees to take the field, Mike nudged Kate. "Maybe one of the Mets players will hit a home run," he said. "Then we'll get to see the Home Run Apple!"

The Home Run Apple was a giant red apple with the Mets logo on it. It was taller than a truck. During games, it stayed hidden in a hole behind center field. But whenever a Mets player hit a home run, the apple rose from its hole.

"That would be cool," Kate said. "*Manzana roja gigante.* Giant red apple." Kate was teaching herself Spanish. Her father knew Spanish because he worked with baseball players from other countries. Kate wanted to be able to speak Spanish like her father, so she practiced whenever she could.

But the Mets didn't hit a home run in the bottom of the first inning. Or the second, third, fourth, or fifth inning. They scored a run by hitting a couple of doubles, but nobody had hit a blast big enough to get a home run. By the bottom of the sixth inning, the Mets were ahead by two. But the fans still wanted a home run.

During the game, Mike and Kate kept an eye on Milo. However, he stayed at his desk, working the whole time.

The first Mets batter of the sixth inning hit a pop fly for an out. The second batter chopped at a curveball and hit a grounder to first for the second out. But the third Mets batter had a full count of three balls and two strikes before he saw his pitch. It was a fastball.

The Mets player swung with all his might.
BLAST!

The bat connected with the ball and sent it flying! The hitter ran for first, and the ball sailed over the outfield wall.

It was a home run!

"Here it comes!" Mike said. He nudged Kate.

Mike and Kate watched as the top of the apple appeared from behind the center-field wall.

But as the apple came out, one of the reporters in the room called out, "Oh no!" Others crowded to the windows to watch.

Mike's and Kate's jaws dropped open.

"That doesn't look like the Home Run Apple I've seen on TV!" Kate said.

Instead of the regular bright red apple with

a Mets logo, the apple that rose from the hole behind center field was very different. It was painted white with dark blue pinstripes that ran top to bottom all around the apple. And there was a giant Yankees logo on the front!

"Someone's pulling a prank on the Mets!" Mike said.

A chorus of *boo*s went up from the Mets fans in the audience, and cheers rose from the Yankees fans. The players milled around on the field while the umpires tried to figure out what to do.

Milo reached for his camera and took a picture. "I can't believe somebody turned the Mets' Home Run Apple into the *Yankees'* Home Run Apple!" he said. "This will make a great scoop!" He walked to his computer and started typing.

"Not so fast," Kate's mother said. She stepped over to the window and took a picture. "My readers will want to see it, too." She tapped on her phone for a moment. "There," she said. "I just sent it to my editor at *America Today* to publish!"

Mike and Kate stared out the window at

the giant pin-striped apple. A few people on the Mets' grounds crew were walking over to it from the infield. Most fans were just staring at the strange sight.

"Can I borrow your binoculars?" Mike asked a nearby reporter. "I want to get a better look."

Up close, Mike could see that the logo on the front of the apple was just a sheet painted with the word *Yankees*. He twirled the dial on the binoculars to zoom out a little bit to see the fans.

"That's strange," Mike said. He nudged Kate. "Use these to look over there." He handed her the binoculars. "At the bottom of the stands just to the right of the Home Run Apple. Do you see that man looking at the apple and talking on a walkie-talkie?"

Kate held the binoculars up to her eyes and scanned the seats near the apple. "Yes," she said. "But it can't be!"

"It is!" Mike said. "He's wearing a Mets jersey and a Yankees cap!"

6

A Hat in the Bag

"We've got to get down there to investigate!" Mike said. "Maybe *he* took the notes, not Milo!"

Kate turned to her mother. "Mom, can we meet you back here in a few minutes? Mike and I want to go see the Yankees' Home Run Apple."

Mrs. Hopkins looked up. "Oh, sure," she said. "I'll be working for the entire game."

"Thanks!" Kate called over her shoulder as she and Mike slipped outside the door of the press box. They ran through the hallways and took an elevator down to the main level. Then they followed the main walkway around the stadium until they found an aisle near the apple.

"There he is!" Mike said, and they ran down the steps toward the field.

The man in the Mets jersey and Yankees hat was standing at the bottom of the aisle. He was too busy talking on his walkie-talkie to notice Mike and Kate racing down the steps.

They stopped just behind him. The nearby fans were still pointing at the big apple.

Kate tapped the man on the shoulder. "Excuse me," she said.

The man jumped and turned around. He had a long face and a beard. His hair was cut in a crew cut.

"Oh!" he said. "Sorry, am I in your way?"

"No," Kate said. She had to talk loudly

because of all the noise from the crowd. Kate pointed to the man's walkie-talkie. "We're just trying to figure out what happened to the Home Run Apple," she said. "We wondered if you knew anything about it."

"I'm afraid I don't," the man said, "even though I should."

"What do you mean?" Mike asked.

The man pointed to the Mets jersey he was wearing. "I'm Rocco Sampson. I work for the Mets," he said. "I'm in charge of pushing the button to make the apple pop up after a home run!"

"That would be fun to do!" Mike said.

"It is," Rocco said. He pointed at the Yankee pinstripes on the apple. "But this isn't fun. Somebody must have done it last night when the stadium was empty."

"Or maybe this afternoon," Kate said.

"Did you hear the press box was broken into? Someone stole my mother's notes!"

"I didn't know that," Rocco said. "But whoever did this was obviously a Yankees fan, not someone who works for the Mets, like me!"

Mike pointed at Rocco's hat. "But what about that?" he asked. "If you work for the Mets, why are you wearing a Yankees hat?"

Rocco smiled. "I wear the Mets jersey and Yankees hat during Subway Series games so I can show I support the crosstown rivalry of Mets and Yankees!" he said. "There's only one thing that makes a good team better, and that's a great opponent!"

"We think whoever stole my mom's notes was also at the Brooklyn Cyclones game this afternoon," Kate said. "The thief left a note for us there. Were you at the game?"

Rocco shook his head. "No," he said. "I was with my boss running errands until about two o'clock today. Then I came back here."

He looked at the apple again. "Sorry, but I've got to go," he said. "I need to figure out how to fix that thing before the next home run."

Rocco reached into his pocket and pulled out a business card and a pen. The card read ROCCO SAMPSON, METS APPLE MANAGER. He flipped it over and wrote on the back *Okay to visit!* and scrawled his signature underneath with a big, looping letter *S*.

"If you're around for the third game of the series, feel free to come visit me in the scoreboard operations room," Rocco said. "Just show the security guard this card and my note on the back. I can show you how the apple works!"

"Wow!" Mike said. He gave Kate a high five. "That would be awesome!"

Rocco smiled, waved goodbye, and headed up to the walkway. As soon as he was out of earshot, Mike looked at Kate.

"I'll bet he took your mom's notes!" he said.

Kate shook her head. "He's got an alibi!" she said. "We can check it out, but if he really was doing errands this morning with his boss, he can't be the person who left us the note at the Cyclones' stadium. We're looking for someone who could have been at the Cyclones game at one o'clock and here by three o'clock."

Mike nodded. "That leaves Milo as our main suspect," he said. "Let's check on him."

Back in the press box, Mike and Kate watched the rest of the first Subway Series game. When the Mets won the game 3–1, Milo finally left his seat to talk to another reporter.

Seeing their chance, Mike and Kate walked over to Milo's chair. As they passed by it, Mike bumped into the chair and knocked the bag onto the ground.

"I've got it," Kate said. She leaned down and picked up the bag, put the Yankees cap back in it, and hung the bag on the chair. "Try to be more careful, Mike!"

"What else was in the bag?" Mike asked as they walked away. "Did you find your mom's notes?"

"Nope! There's nothing in there except the Yankees cap," Kate said. "It's a dead end."

To Catch a Thief?

"Where is he?" Mike asked. "We need to get your mom's notes back!"

It was the next day, just around lunchtime. Mike and Kate were in Monument Park at Yankee Stadium. They were crouched behind a big stone wall.

"Shhh!" Kate said. "We have to hide and be quiet so we can spot him first! Then I can call my mom."

The second Subway Series game was due to start in about an hour. Fans walked through

Monument Park, checking out the plaques and special monuments to famous Yankee players, owners, and managers. A little while before, Mike, Kate, and Mrs. Hopkins had taken the number 4 subway line to Yankee Stadium from their hotel near Grand Central Terminal.

After the first Subway Series game the night before, Mike and Kate had shown Mrs. Hopkins the note and told her their theory about her stolen research. They agreed that Kate and Mike would look for the man at Yankee Stadium before the second game. If they spotted him, Kate would call Mrs. Hopkins in the press box and she'd come down.

Mike and Kate kept an eye on the fans. They were on the lookout for someone in a Mets jersey and a Yankees hat. Out on the field, the Mets were taking batting practice before the game.

"Hey, there's Babe Ruth!" Mike said.

The last time Mike and Kate had visited Yankee Stadium, they solved the mystery of Babe Ruth's ghost.

"That's not Babe Ruth, or even the ghost of Babe Ruth," Kate whispered. She looked at a large red granite stone with the Yankee slugger's name on it. "That's just his monument!"

Mike shrugged. "It still counts as Babe Ruth to me," he said.

They watched one fan after another enter Monument Park through a door at the far end. But none looked like their thief.

"Hey, look!" Mike said. He pointed to a man who had just stepped through the door.

Kate squinted. "That's not him," she said. "He's wearing a Yankees hat *and* shirt! Plus, he doesn't have sunglasses. We have to keep looking."

"Okay," Mike said. "If we can't catch him now, I guess we'll wait until later. Hey, that reminds me. What did the baseball glove say to the ball?"

"I don't know, Mike," Kate said. "What?"

"Catch you later!" Mike whispered. He nudged Kate. "Get it? That's what we're going to do to the thief!"

Kate rolled her eyes. "Ha-ha!" she said. "That's funny. But it's no joke that we need to get my mom's notes back! Let's keep our eyes open!"

They continued to scan the crowd. Since it was almost game time, it was getting busier.

Suddenly, Mike ducked down. "There he is!" he said. "That's got to be him."

Kate glanced at the doorway. A man wearing a Yankees hat and a Mets jersey had just entered the park. He had sunglasses on and dark hair. The man seemed to be looking around at the other fans as if he was searching for someone.

Kate and Mike moved to the far corner of Monument Park and hid behind a group of people.

"Aren't you supposed to call your mom?" Mike asked.

"Let's wait a little bit longer," Kate said. "I want to make sure it's the right person before I call her."

Announcements boomed over the loudspeaker, and fans filled up the seats in the stadium. Mike and Kate kept their eye on the thief as he circled the park. They stayed out of his line of sight, hiding behind the wall or monuments as needed. Finally, he stopped near the front wall and looked at his wrist.

"His watch!" Mike said as he shook Kate's shoulder. "It's silver with a blue and white band. Just like the hot-dog vendor said! It's got to be him!"

"Wow, you're right!" Kate said.

Mike squinted a little. "I can't really see his face, but he reminds me of someone I've seen before. . . ."

Kate nodded. "I know," she said. The man

took off his sunglasses and rubbed his eyes. They could only see the side of his face, but Kate stopped and stared.

"It can't be!" she said. "What's *he* doing here?"

"What do you mean?" Mike asked. "What's *who* doing here? It's the thief! We knew he was going to be here."

Kate stood up. "Let's go!" she said. She started running toward the thief.

"Are you crazy?" Mike asked. "We promised we'd wait for your mom!"

But Kate didn't stop.

Mike jumped up and ran after her. He was just about to grab Kate when the man turned around.

His face broke into a big smile. He opened his arms wide.

Kate sprinted the rest of the way toward the

man. At the last second, she flung out her arms
and wrapped them around the man in a huge
hug. He dropped his sunglasses and hugged
her back.

"Dad!" Kate cried. "I can't believe you're
here!"

A Surprise Visitor

"*¡Hola, papá!*" Kate said. "What are you doing here? I thought you couldn't make it!"

"*Hola,* Kate! My schedule changed and I had a few free days, so I decided to fly out from Los Angeles and surprise you!" her dad said.

"You did!" Kate said. "How did you know we'd be at Monument Park?"

Mr. Hopkins looked from Mike to Kate. "Is that a trick question?" he asked. "I know you love mysteries, so I was hoping you'd figure out the note yesterday at the Cyclones game! I was there, but I couldn't stay to watch you bring out the hot dogs, so I wanted to give you a surprise for the second Subway Series game by meeting you here!"

Kate took a step back. "*You* bought the hot dogs? And *you* left that note for us?" she asked. "We thought it was someone else!"

Mr. Hopkins laughed. "I figured you and Mike would have fun with my riddle. Get it now? I saw you at the Cyclones game, but you didn't see me." He looked at the Yankees plaques and memorials around them. "We're meeting at the monuments, and I just gave you something special—a big hug! And *you* gave *me* a special hug, just like I wrote in the note!"

Mike stepped forward. "We thought *you* were a thief, Uncle Steve!" he said. "Someone took Aunt Laura's notes from the Mets' press box yesterday. The security cameras showed a man with a Yankees hat and Mets jersey, who might have taken them. We thought it was you because that's what the hot-dog vendor said the man who left our note was wearing!"

"Yeah, why are you wearing a Yankees hat?" Kate asked. "You always root for the Mets!"

Mr. Hopkins tilted his hat back. "I do!" he said. "But since your mom loves the Yankees and I was coming for the Subway Series, I figured I ought to support both teams. That's why I picked the different hat and jersey!"

Mike looked around at all the fans exploring Monument Park. "But if *you* didn't take the notes, who did?" he asked.

Mr. Hopkins shrugged. "I'm afraid I don't know," he said. "Maybe you can figure that out when you're back at the Mets' stadium tomorrow. But I *do* know there's a big game about to start. Why don't we get something to eat and then watch the game together?"

Mike started rubbing his belly. "That would be great!" he said. "I've been wanting to try a New York egg cream!" he said.

Kate made a face. "Yuck!" she said. "What's an egg cream? Eggs and cream?"

"Nope. They don't have eggs *or* cream! It's a New York drink. I read about it in the Yankees yearbook," Mike said. "It's got soda water, milk, and chocolate syrup! It sounds yummy!"

Mr. Hopkins laughed. "We'll see what we can find, Mike," he said. "But before we eat, I have to stop by the Yankees' office to drop off a letter."

Mike, Kate, and Mr. Hopkins left Monument Park. They wound their way through Yankee Stadium and took a special elevator to the

Yankees' business office. Once there, they had to sign their names in the visitors' log.

Kate and Mr. Hopkins signed first. Then Mike stepped up to the desk and signed his name in the book while Mr. Hopkins went to the back to drop off his letter.

"Look at that!" Mike said. "I'm an official Yankees visitor! Now I can tell people I made it to the Yankees! I'm going to take a picture."

He pulled out his phone and snapped a picture of the visitors' log. He zoomed in and showed it to Kate.

Kate studied the names in the logbook picture. "Mm-hmm," she said. "Very nice! But that doesn't mean you're on the team, you know."

Mike shrugged. "I know!" he said. "But it's still cool. Just as cool as an *egg cream* would be!"

Mr. Hopkins emerged from dropping off his letter. "Did I hear something about an egg cream?" he asked. "Let's go get one and watch the game!"

As they got ready to leave, Mr. Hopkins pointed to his hat and then his shirt. "I'll be rooting for the Yankees in the first inning and then the Mets in the second inning!"

A Home Run Clue

Mr. Hopkins's plan of rooting for the Yankees in the first inning worked well for the team. The Yankees were on fire! The stadium was full, and the Yankees fans went crazy when the second runner scored to make it 2–0, Yankees.

"I guess they want payback for yesterday's loss," Kate said. "I'm rooting for the Mets, but as long as I'm watching the game with you, Dad, I don't care who wins!"

"And I'm rooting for the Yankees," Mike

said. He took a big slurp of his drink through a red-and-white-striped straw. "But as long as I have my egg cream, I don't care who wins!"

Mr. Hopkins ruffled Mike's hair. "Then I guess we *all* win," he said. "Except for your mother, Kate. What happened to her research?"

As they watched the game, Mike and Kate told Mr. Hopkins how the press box had been broken into and why they had thought it was connected to Mr. Hopkins's mystery note. They also filled him in on their idea that Milo did it.

"I'd bet my plane ticket back to Los Angeles that Milo doesn't have anything to do with it," Mr. Hopkins said. "He's been a friend of your mom's forever."

"Drat!" Kate said to Mike. "If Milo didn't do it, we're at a dead end! He was our only real lead. Our other suspect, Rocco Sampson, has an alibi!"

Even though it wasn't a good day for catching the thief, it was a good day for the Yankees. The Mets just couldn't get ahead in the game. They fought back in the fifth and sixth innings and got two runs. But the Yankees scored one more run in the seventh inning to pull ahead by one.

Nobody scored in the next inning, but the crowd exploded when the Yankees' best hitter, Scooter Boyd, came up to bat with two outs and one runner on base. Mike jumped to his feet with the rest of the fans and clapped. "Come on, Scoot-er! Come on, Scoot-er!" they yelled.

Scooter took a few practice swings and dug his back foot into the dirt. The Mets pitcher fired a fastball straight at home plate.

SWISH!

Scooter swung and missed. But he connected on the very next pitch.

WHAP!

The ball looked like a line drive. As it sailed over the second baseman's outstretched glove, Scooter ran for first. But the ball kept climbing and Scooter kept running. The ball sailed on! It flew over the right-field fence for a home run.

Scooter headed for second base. The other Yankees runner crossed home to score. Scooter crossed home plate with his arms stretched up. Another run for the Yankees! They were ahead by three now. The fans cheered and stomped. It looked like it was going to be a good day for Yankees fans.

Unfortunately for Kate, the Mets didn't stage a rally. After a groundout and two strikeouts in the ninth, the game was over. The Yankees had won. And the Subway Series was tied at one game each. As fans headed for the exits, the song "New York, New York" drifted out of the stadium's loudspeaker.

Some fans swayed and sang along as they left the ballpark.

Mike, Kate, and Mr. Hopkins found their way to the subway station. Kate's mom had to stay in the press box and work after the game, so the kids were going to have dinner with Mr. Hopkins. He'd take them to their hotel later that night.

After a bit of a wait, they pushed onto a number 4 subway train. It was packed with people returning to Manhattan from the game. As the train rumbled along, Mike stared out the windows as trees and buildings rushed by. Kate started to read a Subway Series program she had bought, but then nudged Mike after a few minutes.

"Look! There's Rocco Sampson," she said. Kate pointed to the far end of the subway car.

Standing near the door was the manager of the Mets' Home Run Apple. Just like yesterday, he was wearing a Yankees hat and a Mets jersey. "What's he doing here?" Kate asked.

Mike shrugged. "He's a Mets fan," he said. "He went to the game just like we did!"

Kate studied Rocco. "If he gets off at Grand Central when we do, let's follow him," she said.

A few minutes later, the subway train screeched to a halt at Grand Central, and almost everyone got off. As Mike and Kate stepped onto the platform with Mr. Hopkins, they kept glancing back at Rocco. He had exited the train, too, and was walking behind them in the crowd.

As they wound their way through Grand Central, Mr. Hopkins stopped at an archway in front of the Oyster Bar & Restaurant. The long arches on either side of the walkway were made of glossy marble and curved along the wide tiled ceiling to pillars on all sides.

"Are we going to eat right now?" Mike asked. "That's great! The subway ride made me hungry."

"Soon!" Mr. Hopkins said. "We're going to get takeout and have a picnic dinner in my hotel room. But we can get the food here."

Kate glanced over her shoulder. Rocco was still behind them. He had just taken out his phone.

"Could you get the food, Dad?" she asked. "Mike and I want to hang out here and watch the people."

"Okay," Mr. Hopkins said. "I'll be right back."

Mr. Hopkins headed off to buy dinner. Kate leaned against the glossy marble of one of the archway's pillars. She pretended to flip through the souvenir program she had bought at Yankee Stadium.

As she glanced up from her program, Rocco Sampson walked by. He had his phone pressed against his right ear and was talking to someone.

"There he is!" Mike whispered to Kate. They were just about to follow him when a loud group of girls passed through the hallway.

Rocco stopped walking and put a hand up to cover his left ear. Then he turned to face the wall on the other side of the archway. As soon as he did, Mike and Kate heard a voice in their ears.

"Nope, they didn't suspect anything!" said the voice.

Mike and Kate looked around, but they couldn't tell where the voice was coming from. Kate put a finger to her lips to tell Mike to stay quiet.

"Tomorrow night will be the big game," the voice continued. "I set up a special surprise before the third inning!"

Kate stepped out of the archway to get a better look at the people around them. "Did you hear that?" she asked Mike. "Who was talking?"

"I don't know," Mike said. "Maybe that egg cream is giving us superpowers to hear people's thoughts inside their heads."

"Mike! This is serious!" Kate said.

Far across the passageway, Rocco was still facing the wall and talking into his phone.

"It's him!" she said. "We're hearing what Rocco is saying into his phone!"

Mike frowned. "He's too far away," he said, "and he's facing the wall. It can't possibly be his voice!"

A moment later, the girls finished passing by. Rocco turned back around, slipped the phone into his pocket, and walked up the hallway. The voice stopped.

Kate watched Rocco leave and studied the archway. She grabbed Mike by the shoulders and turned him around so he was facing the archway pillar.

"Wait here," Kate said to Mike. "You can help me test out an idea."

"Hey, it feels like I'm in a time-out!" Mike called from over his shoulder. "No fair!"

Kate ran across the hallway to the other side of the arch. She turned and faced a corner wall of the archway pillar. In a soft voice, she spoke directly into the wall.

"Mike, can you hear me?" she asked.

Mike's voice came out of nowhere. "Loud and clear!"

"That's good," Kate's voice said. "Because I have an idea who took my mom's notes!"

A Mets Fan or a
Yankees Fan?

Kate ran back to Mike.

"Who?" Mike asked. "Who took your mom's notes?"

"Rocco Sampson!" Kate said.

"But we already ruled him out!" Mike said. "He has an alibi, remember? He was doing errands with his boss."

Kate shook her head and smiled. "Nope, he *had* an alibi," she said. "I just figured it out when we heard what he was saying! *'They didn't suspect anything!'* It made me think.

Then I realized his alibi didn't fit any longer!"

"What do you mean?" Mike asked.

"We thought the thief was the same person who left the note for us at the Cyclones game," Kate said. "But *my dad* left the note for us. So the person who stole my mom's notes didn't need to be at the Cyclones game!"

Mike nodded. "So even though Rocco was running errands until two o'clock, he could have been back at the Mets' stadium in time to break into the press box at three o'clock!" he said.

"And I think *that* means we should pay a little visit to the Home Run Apple during tomorrow's game," Kate said. "It sounds like Rocco has something planned for the third inning!"

"It's called the Whispering Gallery," Mr. Hopkins said the next day. Mike, Kate, and

Mr. Hopkins were sitting in front-row seats at the Mets' stadium for the final Subway Series game. "It's a Grand Central secret! When you speak into an arch pillar, the sound gets bounced along the top of the arch, and the person on the other side is able to hear what you say. I'm glad you discovered it!"

"I could use one of those when we're taking a test in school," Mike said. "I could turn around and whisper the question, and Kate could whisper the answer back to me!"

Mr. Hopkins laughed. "I don't think that would be a great way for you to learn, Mike," he said. "It's better to take a test by yourself."

"I know," he said. "But it *would* be a fun way to pull a prank on Mr. Lesch."

"I don't think there's any place you could whisper here and be heard," Kate said.

She was right. It was the bottom of the

second inning of the final Subway Series game, and both the Yankees fans and Mets fans were going crazy. Whichever team won that night would win the series. Neither team had scored yet, but the Mets had one runner on base. Waleed Abdalati, the Mets shortstop, stepped up to the plate.

"Go, Waleed!" Kate shouted. He had hit safely in each of the last ten games.

The first two pitches were high and outside. Waleed didn't swing at either. But the third pitch looked perfect. Waleed unleashed his powerful swing.

WHAP!

The ball flew high into the air. Waleed took off for first base. The ball sailed over the out-field fence. It was a home run! Waleed rounded first and ran for second. As he passed second, the other runner crossed home plate for a run. Then Waleed did, stomping on home plate as he scored!

"Here comes the Home Run Apple!" Mike said. He pointed to center field.

Unlike two days ago, the apple was bright red and had a colorful Mets logo on its front.

"Looks like no one messed around with

it today," Kate said. She snapped a picture of it on her phone.

When she sat back down, Mike nudged her with his elbow. "Now?" he whispered.

"No, not yet," Kate said. "Let's wait until the end of the inning. I'll ask my dad then."

"Okay," Mike said. "Can I see the card he gave us?"

Kate reached into her pocket, pulled out Rocco's business card, and handed it to Mike.

Mike flipped the card over. "Okay to visit!" the message on the back read, with Rocco's signature below.

The looping scrawl of the signature caught his eye. He studied the capital letter *S*. Then he pulled out his phone and found the picture he had taken of his signature in the visitors' book at Yankee Stadium.

Mike scrolled up a little to see the signatures above his. Then he zoomed in and glanced at the back of the business card. The swirly letter S's matched.

"'*Rocco Sampson*'!" he said. "What was Rocco doing at the Yankees' business office?"

"What?" Kate asked.

Mike handed her his phone and the business card. "Look at the signature a few lines above mine," he said. "They're exactly the same!"

Kate stared at the visitors' log and the card.

"Rocco Sampson was in the Yankees' office?" she asked. "But why?"

Mike smiled. He reached over and zoomed in on the right side of the photo. Under the column of the form that said *Reason for Visit*, Rocco had written *interview*.

"Because he was interviewing for a job!" Mike said. "He probably stayed for the game after. That's why we saw him at Grand Central!"

"But he works for the Mets!" Kate said. "He's a Mets fan!"

"He's not a real Mets fan. He's a *Yankees* fan!" Mike said. "*That's* why he was wearing the Yankees hat with his Mets jersey!"

Kate shrugged. "Maybe that's okay," she said. "There's no law against being a Yankees fan!"

"But it's *not* okay to ruin the Mets' Home Run Apple," Mike said. "I'll bet he's the one who painted the pinstripes to support the Yankees! But I don't know why he would have taken your mom's notes."

"We have a lot to investigate!" Kate said.

When the inning ended, Kate talked to her dad and got the okay to go check out the apple with Mike.

But as she and Mike stood up to leave, a

loud "Uh-oh!" rose from the nearby fans. They were pointing to the large video screen on the scoreboard.

Instead of showing game highlights or player information, the screen was showing a video of the Mets' famous mascot, Mr. Met. Mr. Met was a baseball player with a giant baseball for a head. Mets fans love Mr. Met, but they didn't love this video!

Loud choruses of *boo*s rose up from the crowd. A smattering of Yankees fans cheered, but they were drowned out by the Mets fans' negative reactions.

Streaming across the giant scoreboard screen were videos of a Mr. Met bobblehead toy encountering trouble. The first video showed Mr. Met falling out of a tree and smashing to pieces. The second video showed

Mr. Met being covered by teddy bears with Yankees jerseys. The third video seemed to show a New York Yankees sock monkey dropping Mr. Met in a toilet!

A Real Subway Series Catch!

Mike and Kate stopped in their tracks and watched the videos. Yankees fans were cheering, and Mets fans were booing.

"Some Yankees fan must have hacked into the Mets' scoreboard!" Mike said. "Boy, they'll do anything to get the Mets!"

Mr. Hopkins shook his head. "That might rile up the fans, but it's going to take more than a few silly videos to throw the Mets off tonight," he said. "I *know* it's their night to win!"

"Don't be so sure of that, Mr. H," Mike said.

"The Yankees are the real winners in New York City! Check the World Series statistics!"

Mr. Hopkins smiled and gave Mike a fist bump. "We'll see about that tonight!" he said.

A moment later, the videos stopped and the announcer's voice boomed over the loudspeaker. "Sorry for the video problem," he said. A picture of the Home Run Apple appeared on the screen. "We'll be back to the game shortly!"

Kate tugged on Mike's T-shirt. "See you in a little bit, Dad," she said. "We're going to check out the apple."

Kate's dad waved goodbye, and Mike and Kate bounded up the steps to the walkway. Mike followed Kate as they wound their way through the Mets' stadium to the scoreboard operations room. Kate showed the security guard the business card and Rocco's signature, and the guard waved them into a long hallway.

"It's the second door on the left," she said.

Just before they reached the door, Kate stopped Mike. "Remember, we have to find my mom's notes," she said. "If he took them, they might be in his office."

Mike knocked softly on the white door labeled SCOREBOARD OPERATIONS. While he waited, he rolled his baseball from hand to hand. A moment later, Rocco opened the door.

"Hey! Hello again!" he said. "You just missed a home run! You could have watched me press the button. Come on in."

Mike and Kate walked into the control room. It was filled with computer screens and TV monitors. Windows looked out onto the field and scoreboard. Two other people sat at the far end of the room behind keyboards, with headsets on.

"Mike and Kate, right?" Rocco asked.

Kate nodded. "Thanks for letting us stop by," she said. "This is pretty neat." She scanned the room and noticed a desk in the corner with a miniature Home Run Apple on it. Underneath the desk were piles of paper.

Rocco led them over to a control panel filled with lights and buttons. He pointed to a silver lock mounted on the panel. A key was inserted into the lock.

"There's the control for the apple," he said. "After we verify that the Mets have hit a home run, I use the key to turn that lock." Rocco pointed to a nearby black switch. "Once the lock is turned, I flip open the cover of this switch. When I press the button underneath, the Home Run Apple pops up!"

"Cool!" Mike said. "Can I take a picture?"

"Sure," Rocco said.

Mike handed Kate his baseball and took a

picture of the lock and the switch. "I'd love to have a button like that so I could press it and have it do my homework!" he said.

"Is that all you can think of?" Kate asked as she handed the baseball back.

Mike paused for a moment. "No...," he said. He rubbed his tummy. "I can also think of a button that I could press and have apple pie pop up from my kitchen counter. That would be nice!"

"Mmmm...," Kate said. "I like apple pie, too. Maybe the button can deliver *two* slices!"

Rocco laughed. "We don't have that kind of button here," he said. "But it sounds tasty." He walked toward another area of the room. "Here, let me show you how the scoreboard works."

Mike started to follow him, but Kate

nudged him with her elbow. She glanced at Rocco's desk.

Mike followed her eyes. He gave her a thumbs-up and motioned for her to follow Rocco. As she walked behind Rocco, Mike rolled his baseball from hand to hand again. But as he transferred the ball, Mike let it slip. He gave it a little tip so it would roll toward Rocco's desk.

BONK! The ball bounced across the floor, and then rolled to a stop under the desk.

"Sorry!" Mike said. "I'll get it."

Rocco brought Kate over to another set of computer screens. While he started to explain how they put the score up, Mike crawled under Rocco's desk. He dug through the pile of papers on the floor. Underneath some old baseball magazines were printouts of the scores of

baseball games. Finally, near the bottom, he spotted something different.

Kate was pointing at the scoreboard and asking Rocco questions. Mike reached down and pulled out a stack of notebook papers from the pile.

He glanced at the top page, grabbed his ball, and scrambled out from under the desk. He walked over to where Rocco was pointing at buttons on the control panel and then pointing to the scoreboard.

"Rocco?" Mike said. "I found my baseball under your desk. But I also found this."

Mike held up the stack of notebook papers. The top page read PROPERTY OF LAURA HOPKINS.

"Why do you have my mom's notes?" Kate asked.

New York, New York!

Rocco Sampson stared at Mike.

"I don't know what you're talking about," Rocco said.

"Yes, you do," Kate said. "You stole my mother's notes from the press box two days ago. And you're the one who painted the Home Run Apple with Yankees pinstripes. You even told us that you knew the stadium would be empty the night before the first game. I'll bet you snuck in and painted it yourself!"

"And you're probably the one who hacked

into the scoreboard with all those videos of Mr. Met," Mike said.

Rocco leaned back against the chair in front of the scoreboard controls. "You can't prove any of that," he said.

"Actually, we do have proof," Mike said. "We heard you talking on the phone last night in Grand Central. You said that you set up a special surprise for the third inning!"

"And we can prove another important thing," Kate said. She borrowed Mike's phone and pulled up the picture of the visitors' log from Yankee Stadium.

"You're a Yankees fan!" Kate said. "You were there interviewing for a job yesterday. You're pulling all these pranks on the Mets because you're a Yankees fan."

Rocco stared at the picture and the pile of stolen papers that Mike was holding. Then he pulled out the chair and dropped into it. He let out a long sigh.

"You're right," he said softly. "I did steal your mom's notes, along with other stuff from the press box. And I did all those other things, too."

"But why?" Mike asked.

Rocco shrugged. "Just because I *work* for the Mets doesn't mean I *like* the Mets," he said. "I've always loved the Yankees, but I couldn't get a job with them. So I settled for a job with the Mets. But I kept applying to work with the Yankees. I knew they were going to hire me this time, so I wanted to pull some pranks on the Mets before I left. It was the perfect opportunity for a Yankees fan!"

"But why did you steal my mom's notes?" Kate asked. "What does she have to do with this?"

"Nothing," Rocco said. "I just broke into the press box to confuse the investigators. I didn't want to steal anything valuable. I figured I would take a few books or notebooks and make it seem like whoever painted the apple also tried to rob the place. That would throw suspicion off me."

Kate crossed her arms and stared at Rocco. "Well, that was a bad idea," she said. "You stole from the wrong person. Mike and I can figure out any mystery. Especially when it's my mom who's missing something!"

Mike and Kate tracked down Emma at the Mets' security office. They told her the whole story. Emma thanked them for being so clever and set out to find Rocco and investigate.

"I'll make sure he doesn't pull any more

pranks on the Mets," Emma said as they left.
"Or steal anything else!"

Mike and Kate returned to their seats to
watch the rest of the game with Mr. Hopkins
and told him everything. The fifth inning
was over, and the Mets had pulled ahead by
three runs. The Yankees couldn't find the
magic they had the night before. By the time
the ninth inning rolled around, the Mets were
ahead by two. Although the Yankees got two

runners on base, the next two batters struck out. Mike and the other Yankees fans in the stadium cheered loudly for Scooter Boyd when he stepped to the plate with two outs and two runners on base.

But he lofted a weak pop fly on his first bat. The Mets shortstop caught it, and the game was over. The Mets had won the third Subway Series game, and they also won the series, two games to one! The fans exploded with cheers and shouts. Kate and Mr. Hopkins high-fived. "Way to go, Miracle Mets!" Kate said.

Mike shrugged and waved his hand. "Don't get too excited," he said. "It's just one series. I'm sure the Yankees will win next time! After all, they have a pretty good record."

When the fans thinned out, Mike, Kate, and Mr. Hopkins went to the press box to meet Mrs. Hopkins.

When they spotted her, Mike and Kate ran over, gave her the notebook pages they had found under Rocco Sampson's desk, and explained how they had caught him. Mrs. Hopkins was speechless. She gave both of them a big hug!

"I can't believe you caught the thief by overhearing him at the Whispering Gallery at Grand Central!" Mrs. Hopkins said. She shuffled through the notebook pages. "Thank you so much for finding my notes! Now I'll be able to finish my book on time."

When Mrs. Hopkins was done working, the four of them left the stadium and took the number 7 subway train back to Grand Central Terminal. Kate's parents led Kate and Mike through the passageways until they emerged onto Forty-Second Street.

"Well, I've got to head back to Los Angeles

tomorrow," Mr. Hopkins said. "And the three of you have to get back to Cooperstown. But we have one more night together in New York City. Who'd like to go up in the Empire State Building?"

Mike raised his hand and jumped up and down. "I would, Uncle Steve!" he said.

"*Ooh!* I would, too!" Kate said. "But I want to be the Statue of Liberty first!"

Mr. Hopkins looked at his watch. "I'm afraid we don't really have time to see the Statue of Liberty on this trip," he said. "Maybe next time."

"No!" Kate said. "I don't want to *see* the Statue of Liberty—I want to *be* it!"

Mr. and Mrs. Hopkins looked at Kate. "Are you feeling okay, Kate?" her mom asked. "Maybe we've seen too many baseball games."

Kate smiled. She pointed to a booth across

the street. The sign on the front read:

BE THE STATUE OF LIBERTY!
COME TRY THE NEW YORK PHOTO EXPERIENCE.
TAKE HOME A PICTURE OF YOU
AS YOUR FAVORITE NEW YORK SIGHT!

Mr. Hopkins laughed. "Okay, we have time for that before the Empire State Building," he said.

The photo booth had all types of special costumes and props so that visitors could take New York–themed pictures of themselves as souvenirs. A few minutes later, Kate had pulled on a green robe and put a large spiked foam crown on her head. She had a stone tablet in one hand and held a torch up high in her other, just like the Statue of Liberty.

But before the woman at the photo booth

could snap a picture, Mike jumped in front of the camera. "Hang on!" he said. "I've got a better idea!"

Mike ran over to the shelves stocked with different photo props and pulled out a baseball glove. He ran back to Kate and swapped the baseball glove for her torch. Then he swapped out the tablet Kate was holding with the Subway Series program she had bought at the baseball game.

"What am I supposed to do with this?" Kate asked as she looked at the baseball glove.

"Just hold it up like the torch," Mike said. "You'll see!"

Kate sighed. She cradled the Subway Series program in her left hand and held up the baseball glove instead of the Statue of Liberty's torch with her right.

Just as the attendant was getting ready to

snap the picture, Mike tossed his baseball up. The ball sailed in an arc in front of Kate.

SNAP!

The attendant took a picture.

THWUMP!

Mike's ball landed right in Kate's glove!

"Woohoo!" Mike cried. "That was the greatest New York City Subway Series catch of all time!"

Dugout Notes

☆ Subway Series ☆

New York Mets. The Mets are a National League team. They started in 1961, as an expansion team to replace the New York Giants and Brooklyn Dodgers, both of which had left for California in the late 1950s. In their first season, the Mets had a record of 40 wins and 120 losses, one of the worst regular season records of all time. They finished last or second-to-last every year until 1969, when they won the World Series. That year they were known as the Miracle Mets because they beat the Baltimore Orioles in a huge upset.

New York Yankees. The Yankees are an American League team. They actually started out in Baltimore in 1901 as the Baltimore Orioles. Then they moved to New York and became the New York Highlanders. Finally the team took the name the New York Yankees in 1913. They have won more division titles, pennants, and World Series than any other baseball team. Over the years, they have had many famous players, including Derek Jeter, Reggie Jackson, Babe Ruth, Lou Gehrig, Joe DiMaggio, Mickey Mantle, Yogi Berra, Whitey Ford, and more. Their biggest rivals are the Boston Red Sox and the New York Mets.

Subway Series. A Subway Series is a series of baseball games between two New York City teams, since fans can reach the stadiums via subway trains. The first Subway Series were played as World Series games. For example, the Yankees played the New York Giants in 1921, and the Brooklyn Dodgers in 1941. More recently, the

Mets and the Yankees have been playing Subway Series games during the regular season. They typically play groups of two or three games at each team's stadium. The Mets and the Yankees competed in a World Series Subway Series in 2000, and the Yankees won in five games.

Yankee Stadium. Yankee Stadium is in the area of New York City called the Bronx. It opened in 2009 and replaced the original Yankee Stadium, which opened in 1923, when Babe Ruth was on the team. Many years ago, Monument Park was actually located in the outfield, in play! Players had to avoid the monuments while fielding baseballs. The Yankees moved it behind the outfield fence in the 1970s. When they moved it to the new Yankee Stadium, they put it behind the center-field wall.

Mets' stadium. The Mets' stadium, known as Citi Field, is in the area of New York City called Queens. It opened in 2009 and replaced Shea Stadium, which opened in 1964. For their first two seasons, the Mets played at the Polo Grounds, a stadium used mainly for baseball and football. The Mets' stadium is in Flushing Meadows, a large park that was the site of the World's Fair in

1939 and again in 1964. The Unisphere, a giant globe built for the fair, is still a tourist attraction.

Mets' stadium features. The Mets' stadium has some interesting features. There's a Mets Hall of Fame near the entrance, which has information on famous players, important games, and Mets history. It even has the original Mr. Met mascot costume! The main entrance to the stadium is the Jackie Robinson Rotunda, a large circular area dedicated to Jackie Robinson's life and accomplishments. And there really is a Home Run Apple. The apple is sixteen feet tall and eighteen feet wide!

Number 4 and 7 trains. Yankees fans can take the number 4 train or the B or D train. The number 4 subway train runs through Grand Central Terminal to Yankee Stadium, at the 161st Street/Yankee Stadium stop. Mets fans take the number 7 train, which travels through Grand Central Terminal to the Mets' stadium, at the Mets/Willets Point stop.

Whispering Gallery. There really are whispering arches in Grand Central Terminal, as well as in many other buildings. Whispering galleries, arches, or walls can be found around the world, from St. Paul's Cathedral in London to the U.S. Capitol in Washington, D.C., to Union Station in St. Louis. Typically, the stone or tiles on the arch plus the shape of the arch or dome itself cause sounds to be carried by waves, known as whispering-gallery waves, from one side of the arch to the other.

MOST VALUABLE PLAYERS
MVP

MOST VALUABLE PLAYERS
MVP
THE GOLD MEDAL MESS

DAVID A. KELLY AUTHOR OF THE BALLPARK Mysteries

★
Always show spirit!
★
Bring their all to any sport!
★
Never give up!
★

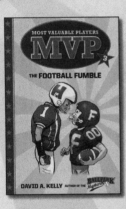

MOST VALUABLE PLAYERS
MVP 3
THE FOOTBALL FUMBLE

DAVID A. KELLY AUTHOR OF THE BALLPARK Mysteries

MOST VALUABLE PLAYERS
MVP 2
THE SOCCER SURPRISE

DAVID A. KELLY AUTHOR OF THE BALLPARK Mysteries

A NEW SERIES FROM THE AUTHOR OF THE

BALLPARK
Mysteries

MOST VALUABLE PLAYERS
MVP 4
THE BASKETBALL BLOWOUT

DAVID A. KELLY AUTHOR OF THE BALLPARK Mysteries

1256

RandomHouseKids.com   RHCB

New friends. New adventures.
Find a new series ... just for you!

Isadora Moon: Cover art © by Harriet Muncaster. Commander in Cheese: Cover art © by AG Ford. Julian's World: Cover art © by Robert Papp. Puppy Pirates: Cover art © Luz Tapia. Purrmaids: Cover art © by Andrew Farley. Ballpark Mysteries: Cover art © by Mark Meyers.

ISADORA MOON

For ballerina and fairy and vampire lovers

COMMANDER IN CHEESE

For adventurers

JULIAN'S WORLD
THE STORIES JULIAN TELLS

For storytellers

PUPPY PIRATES

For dog lovers

PURRMAIDS

For mermaid and cat lovers

BALLPARK Mysteries

For sports fans

RHCB **RHCBooks.com**